For Freya, Torfi, Magnus and Ronja, with love xxx – V.F.

To Chris, with love – C.F.

OXFORD
UNIVERSITY PRESS
Great Clarendon Street, Oxford OX2 6DP

Oxford University Press is a department of the University of Oxford.
It furthers the University's objective of excellence in research,
scholarship, and education by publishing worldwide in

Oxford   New York

Auckland   Cape Town   Dar es Salaam   Hong Kong   Karachi
Kuala Lumpur   Madrid   Melbourne   Mexico City   Nairobi
New Delhi   Shanghai   Taipei   Toronto

With offices in

Argentina   Austria   Brazil   Chile   Czech Republic   France   Greece
Guatemala   Hungary   Italy   Japan   Poland   Portugal   Singapore
South Korea   Switzerland   Thailand   Turkey   Ukraine   Vietnam

Oxford is a registered trade mark of Oxford University Press
in the UK and in certain other countries

Text © Vivian French 2006
Illustrations © Chris Fisher 2006

British Library Cataloguing in Publication Data available

ISBN-13: 978-0-19-279086-6 (Hardback)
ISBN-10: 0-19-279086-2 (Hardback)
ISBN-13: 978-0-19-272538-7 (Paperback)
ISBN-10: 0-19-272538-6 (Paperback)

10 9 8 7 6 5 4 3 2 1

Printed in Singapore

Little Dog

Little Dog

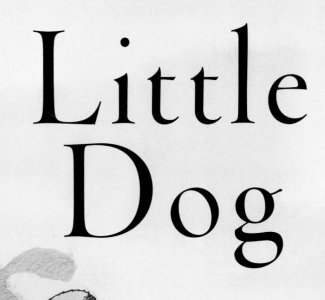

Vivian French

illustrated by Chris Fisher

OXFORD
UNIVERSITY PRESS

Little Dog and **Big Dog** were going
to see Great Aunt M.

'Can I hold your hand?' Little Dog asked.
'No,' said Big Dog.
'Holding hands is soppy.'
Little Dog hugged Froggie.
'Froggie doesn't like Great Aunt M's house,'
he said. 'He doesn't like the *hairies*.'
They climbed the steps. The front door was open.

'WOWLY! WOWLY! WOWLY! WOO! WOO! WOO!'

Three **enormous** hairies came tumbling towards them.

'OH OH OH!' cried Little Dog.
'Don't be frightened, dear Little Dog,'
said Great Aunt M. 'The hairies won't hurt you.'
She picked Little Dog up and
carried him inside.

'Where's Froggie?'
whispered Little Dog.
'I want my Froggie.'
Nobody heard him.

'Can we have our tea now?' asked Big Dog.

'It's all ready, my dear ones,' said Great Aunt M.

'YUM YUM!' said Big Dog.

Little Dog looked at the biscuits.

'Froggie likes biscuits,' he said, and his voice wobbled.

'So do I,' said Big Dog, and he ate four biscuits very quickly indeed.

'Wouldn't you like some chocolate cake, Little Dog?'
said Great Aunt M.

Little Dog shook his head. *'I want my Froggie,'*
he said.
'I LOVE chocolate cake,' said Big Dog,
and he ate **three** large slices.
Little Dog was so worried about Froggie that
he stood on his tippytoes and waved his arms.

‘I want to look for Froggie NOW!’

Great Aunt M nodded.
'In a minute, my precious.'

Little Dog hurried to the window
and peered out.

The hairies were lying in a snuffling, snoring heap.
Something green and floppy lay beside them.
'FROGGIE!' Little Dog shouted.

'They've got my Froggie!'

Little Dog crept down the steps.
One of the hairies snored. A long, rumbling, fearsome snore.
Froggie looked very small and crumpled between its paws.

'You WON'T eat my Froggie!'
Little Dog whispered fiercely. 'I won't let you!'

Little Dog took a deep breath. He began to tiptoe across the grass. His heart was pounding, and his tummy felt funny.

'N...N...Nearly there,'

he said to himself,

'I'm nearly there...'

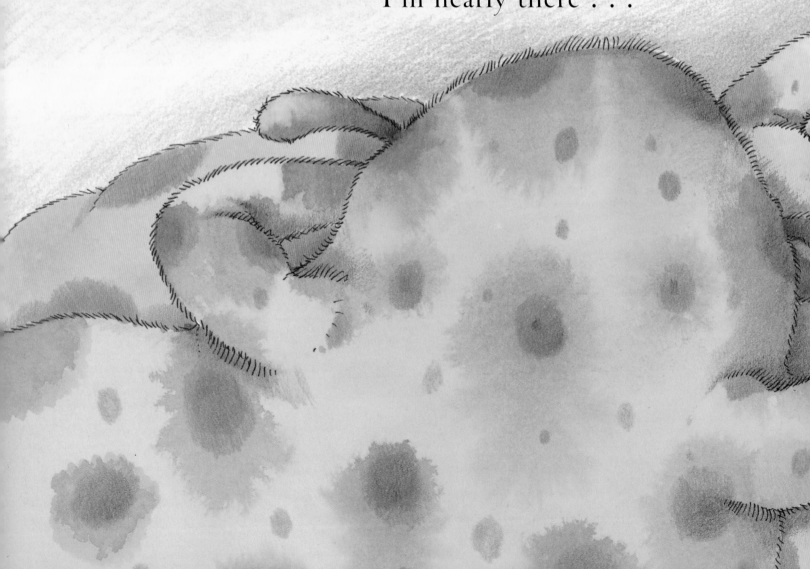

'WOWLY! WOWLY! WOWLY! WOO! WOO! WOO!'

The hairies L^EA^PT up.

Little Dog snatched at Froggie, but the biggest hairy grabbed Froggie's dangling leg and began to pull.

'LET MY FROGGIE GO!'
SHOUTED Little Dog, and he STAMPED his foot.
The biggest hairy dropped Froggie,
and all the hairies stared.

Little Dog ran for the door, hugging Froggie tightly.

He flung himself at Great Aunt M.
'LOOK! LOOK!
I SAVED Froggie!'

And he helped himself to *the last* slice of chocolate cake.

'*Humph,*' said Big Dog,
'it's time to go home.'
And he opened the door.

'WOO! WOO! WOWLY! WOO!'
The hairies came rushing in.
Big Dog *jumped* behind Great Aunt M.

Little Dog froze, but the hairies rolled on the ground in front of him and licked his toes and purred.

'*WOW!*' Big Dog stared.

'They really like *you*!'

Little Dog tucked Froggie safely under his arm.
He looked at the hairies, and took a
small
step
forward.

'I like them too,' he said.
And he patted them one by one.

'But Froggie is still my . . .

BESTEST friend . . .'